What Had Become of Us

Fiction by Kathryn Kuitenbrouwer
All the Broken Things (2014)
Perfecting (2009)
The Nettle Spinner (2005)
Way Up (2003)

KATHRYN KUITENBROUWER

What Had Become of Us

GOOSE LANE EDITIONS

"What Had Become of Us" previously appeared in Kathryn Kuitenbrouwer's 2003 story collection, *Way Up*, published by Goose Lane Editions.

Pieter Van Dongen and I were in another forest completely, and not surprisingly, my life had changed irrevocably and in subtle ways that I did not necessarily wish to examine. The acknowledging of change in any way brought with it a tenderness, a weepiness, a general atmosphere of misery that I would sooner deny. The forest in which we stood had been ravaged by a hurricane. Very few trees had survived the winds. It was a year to the day since Erwin's death.

What are we supposed to do here? I asked.

Cleaning up, Pieter said.

I had come to Belgium in order to leave Canada. It was as simple and as complicated as that could be. I wanted to leave home, family — a family I suspected of subversive politeness and congeniality, which was okay if you liked that sort of thing, but I had decided that on the whole I didn't — and seek the sort of autonomy that I expected might be found in the arms of a foreigner, on foreign terrain, in the imagined, nuanced otherness of a stranger's bed, in heavily accented intercourse. I had dreams — vivid sleeping dreams — that assured me this was possible, and so I sought, in my naivety, a non-Canadian boyfriend, a saviour from a far-off land, someone cultivated, if possible, but certainly non-English speaking. I had no desire for argument.

I met Pieter in a dingy university bar in the oldest section of Ghent. It was full of miserable intellectuals for the most part, people who snorted instead of laughed, as if they were entirely above humour. He was different, of course, else I'd never have bothered with him. He was all gangly and confident. He had a small logging operation. It was hard to imagine anyone logging in Belgium, and so I found him generally amusing, archaic; I suppose I fell in love with him almost immediately. He spoke a disjointed, dysfunctional English, which made everything he said sound charming and vaguely stupefied.

You like me. I like you. We are aliking each other, he said. Is this good?

Do you hire women on your logging crews? I asked this demurely and out of pure tactic. We were standing beside each other at the bar, drinking blanchkes with little peels of lemon sinking down into them. It was obvious I was having him on; I was a terrible flirt. Of course, I was over there with only one goal in mind. I could be very stubborn, a real stickler for goals and such. He was adorable, all standing-up hair and questioning eyes, clean-shaven. He stared at me, not understanding the question.

I repeated, Do you ever have women working for you?

Oh, no, never, he said.

Really? I'm very strong.

Yes, oh, I would hire you, Adriana. This is special.

That was how it started. An enormous amount of time had passed since. Pieter's English had come to be letter perfect; I had come to see that the goal of autonomy was a shifting bastard of a thing. That ideal of self, a container of you-ness or me-ness, was a facile improbability, as all ideals are. I was not unhappy; I was hurtling toward happiness at all times. I had attained some sort of freedom — the sort given by your loved ones even as they cleave to you. Maybe that's all a person could expect.

I wished I had slept with Erwin before he died, before Pieter felled the spindly little scrap of a tree that would decapitate him and end his days on earth. They were brothers, you know. I wish I had the pleasure and misery of certain memories of Erwin's hand along the inside of my thigh, the surfacing of orgasm like a shattering of any possibility. I could languish in the grudge that the widow bears the dead and the almost-faux secret the adulteress coddles from her husband (for he must know, he must). My miscreant behaviour would not have been against Pieter. I would have slept with Erwin in spite of my love for Pieter, in spite of myself and all common sense, in spite of Erwin, who no doubt would have had his own good reasons for not crossing the line, yet could not, just as I could not, forestall the fates.

The poplar trees in this mess of a forest all these years later had been planted in 1946 under the instruction of the Belgian government, once the ash from the Second World War had settled. The distance between each of these trees, the distance between all trees in Belgium, was set at eight metres. The undergrowth was grassy where it wasn't overgrown with stinging nettle or damped down by rotting leaves. A recent hurricane had spun the tops of the trees viciously in twisted circles and back on themselves, plucked them out of the earth like so many weeds and thrown them down like little sticks on top of each other. Their trunks flexed unnaturally; some of these trees were thirty metres in height (now length), and the torque buildup in their stems was enormously dangerous if you happened to want to try to trim the branches, cut the roots away, clean the butt end, and chop the leaders off, which is exactly what we intended to do. We expected the trees to violently resist our taming.

This one's for Erwin, Pieter said. He dedicated every forest he felled or cleaned up to his brother, as if an accumulation of offerings would alter the course of history. I watched the chimney stack of the Doem nuclear station off to the left, far in the distance, its smoke billowing in a cumulus of waste and condensation. The infrastructure for the building was largely underground; the stack was huge. They were having problems with fish — herring mostly — being drawn into the reactor by the tens of thousands. They were drawn through the water intake into the heavy water tanks. Pieter and Erwin used to slide herring down their throats, whole.

These are fantastic, Adriana. Open up.

Yes, open up, Erwin had said, forcing me to sit and then pulling my head back, making me laugh so that he could bring a fish down over my tongue. I gagged on the salty ocean meat; he held his open palm along my throat.

Hollanders and the people of the lowlands have a great love for herring. They smoke by the millions those caught off the coast in the cold currents of the North Sea, and what is more, they pickle the rest and can them in attractive little aluminum tins, the lids of which peel off with the help of a sort of Allèn key. They stand at market, and have done so for centuries, in little manly groups, tilting their heads back and sliding the fish down their gullets. It is a tradition — men in wooden clompen and blue marine sweaters (knitted in cables and tied with effeminate pompoms at the neck), their throats translucently white, like swans swallowing. The Doem laboratories subcontracted the job, installing underwater screens and noisemakers to keep the herring in safe water. A loud, dull, unfriendly din was broadcast beneath the sea, and still the herring were awed by the sucking intake toward the heavy water containers. Some slipped through the protective mesh. The rest huddled, their noses bumping again and again into the screen, listening to the whirr of eradication.

Pieter and Erwin had been singing a song, and when they finished, they rolled open a tin of little dead fishes and laughed at my disgust and slid them into their mouths. I felt Erwin's hand undulate along the shape of the fish, creating space in my esophagus; his fingertips ran slightly under my sweater. I could have left Pieter in our bed that night and gone to him — his hand would run down my throat, my hand would draw his foreskin down, we should kiss then, a line of spittle between our tongues.

Pieter had introduced me to Erwin within days of my arrival in Ghent.

He's better than me in every way.

Erwin was a tall, tousle-haired dirty blond with a cheeky smile and a lanky off-kilter walk, like an overgrown child. He was not better in any way than Pieter but rather was a sort of complement, as if the two brothers, so close in age, had taken only certain human aspects and nurtured them but left the rest to rot, knowing that the other would compensate. We ate together every night — we called these meals *homemade primitives* — stews or omelettes, spaghetti. Once we dumped osso bucco unceremoniously on the table, no plates or cutlery, salad scattered in the centre. We ate like that to alleviate the banality of life and because it made us laugh. We drank plonk directly out of the bottle and laughed and laughed.

Erwin's death precipitated a personality gap in Pieter, of course, a void which initially filled with sorrow. I believe that death became a strange life force in our relationship. The actions of our daily lives were a direct result of our sadness; we were affected, I say touched, by that ghost of loss.

He's not coming back, I said.

I don't expect it, either.

But you wish.

He said, There is a crooner song Erwin and I used to sing — I piss like before in the sink/ I sleep with my clothes on/ what a lousy life.

So, you don't even wish it.

It's like this, I think, he said as he sat down on a fallen tree trunk, which bounced like a park toy. I don't expect it, and I don't wish it. It's over. But still a part of me looks over my shoulder and recognizes him in other people, as if he has scattered — little atoms and molecules seeking a place in this stranger's hair colour, that one's glint of the eye. He has become a series of lost pieces.

I took a swig from Pieter's thermos. It was not coffee. The wine was bitter at first, its sweetness hidden within this cold unhappiness. I took comfort in Pieter, in his body — his handsome face which was vaguely flattened out, his high cheekbones; he was older in appearance than in reality. The muscles in his back extended up into his convex neck, giving his head a look of stability. His hair was golden in the diffused Flemish light. His lips had a curving sensuality. Weather had given his forehead a furrow of concern; he had an elegant body curving into natural muscles, his penis a fascinating exclamation mark.

He had been working the forests across Belgium for more than ten years. We sat quietly there on the lopped branch for some time beside a line of Stihl chainsaws, a can of oil, a can of gasoline. I wondered about it, about the atomic dispersal of Erwin. The arc of Pieter's penis, had it changed, shifted from left to right, lightened slightly in hue? There were still parts of his body unexplored. I made a mental note to slow down, take my time about it. A waft of gasoline blew past on the wind, sweet.

When's the crane supposed to be here?

By noon.

Do you have a plan?

It's going to be a day from hell, I can tell you.

As far as the eye could see, not a tree was left standing. The wreckage hung limp from upturned root systems or snapped right off. The jagged, splintered wood was a pale, sap-shiny yellow. I climbed down into a crater, the negative space where the roots of a tree had been. The earth beneath was muddy. I lifted my boots, pumped the squelching mess and enjoyed the sensation of suction resistance.

If you cut off the stem now, I'll be buried alive.

Come out.

Come in and see what it feels like.

No, Adriana.

I looked up into the gnarled mess of roots and earth. Larvae wriggled back in. Little shards of coloured glass, old detritus reflected the sun back at me.

Hey, look at this.

It's an old landfill, a dump, that's all.

Look, there's a road for little creatures here, along the roots and between them, coming up along the surface.

What do you see in these worms? Anything hopeful?

What could be more hopeful than death and decay? Do me a favour and cut off that damn stem. I won't feel a thing.

Pieter said, I have work to do.

The trees had swayed in the autumn breeze

just one week before. The leaves had just begun to react to the lessening light, to turn yellow and brown and to fall. Small animals had hoarded food here. Children had played in this forest, screamed laughing, running away from imagined predation. Adults had nestled into the composting leaves and swayed to more primal necessities, in lieu of love. A forester had made the rounds, a shotgun slapping his green-corduroyed thigh, a spaniel at his side.

We'd been caught once, Pieter and I, in flagrante delicto, by the brindle hondt, the water dog that every forester seemed to own. The snuffling, cold snout had alerted us in time to hastily clothe ourselves and appear unflushed, deep into our lovemaking as we had been.

Goeie Morgen, the forester had said.

And to you, I replied.

You're English, he said.

Canadian.

Then he noticed and spluttered, Why, you're a girl!

I had flicked the switch on my Stihl 64 and pulled the cord; the machine roared to life. I nodded at him by way of excusing myself and got to work, using the chainsaw as a sort of machete, clearing the bramble and nettle from around the closest tree. I was wet between the legs. Pieter and I were in the bower of our love affair then, the first month. I cannot imagine making love out of doors now except as an act of pretense or desperation.

Lately, our lovemaking had taken on the sobriety of a Mass, of a wound healing; it was a communion of sadness. And we drew Erwin into even that. In the dampness of our bed, humid and hot, we talked of nothing else.

How could you, I mean, in that big forest, with all that space around. One man is so small.

I don't know how it happened.

You don't know?

It's a mess right now, Adriana. In my head. Did I do it on purpose without meaning to do it on purpose — fantasy out of control? A waking dream? I wish I had done it on purpose. It would make sense then.

Pieter, I wasn't suggesting that. I meant something about probabilities. Space and motion and mathematics. The field was so big, the tree so small, that kind of thing.

I felled the tree into an empty space. Then, there he was.

Are you suggesting...? I whispered even though there were only the two of us in the house.

Inconceivable, he said.

The tree that killed Erwin was not really worth chopping. At less than half a cubic metre of useable wood, it didn't look as if it could kill a fly. Erwin didn't see it coming, felt, as they say, not a thing. His life did not flash before his eyes, not that that's any consolation. He died instantly. Pieter shouted and ran, but it was too late. He held him, held him as if he could, like making a puzzle, reunite his body with his body. I was not there. I had taken the day off because my birthday was coming up and I wanted to have a day to myself. I had gone to purchase an album of Bulgarian vocal music. I had it on the turntable at top volume when Pieter came home, his hands bloodied, the tattered quilted workshirt he wore soaked through with Erwin's stuff; bits of brain matter and wood chips clung where the flannel shirt had worn through, the cotton insulation spilling out. The nuances of the Bulgarian's song, the layers of complex vocal arrangement were already forming into something unreliable, some memory we could try to grasp later to force sense out of the senseless.

You could have pushed the tree sideways.

I didn't... it didn't occur to me.

No. I just wondered. If he'd been just paralyzed...

He would have hated that.

We could wheel him around in a chair, I said. I thought about his helpless body, about undressing him, the heavy useless limbs, the limp curve of spine, like dead but not, just not.

With every tree he cut down, Pieter's body took on the shape of the stem. He leaned into his work in a kind of yearning posture. He rose as the tree passed its centre and began its fall. Then he shifted and stood and watched it fall, often pulling out his Drum tobacco to roll a cigarette even as the trunk crashed to earth. When the back of Erwin's skull broke away, when Pieter saw the brain was crushed and bits of bone had shattered like china into the mess of his brother, he did all he could. He acted pragmatically, picked up the cap of Erwin's skull and fitted it back as well as he could manage, unaware of the blood spillage. He nestled Erwin's head into his own lap, holding him together for some time, as if time would heal all wounds. Pieter kept his focus on Erwin's face;

he claimed it took on an otherworldly beauty. He drew his hand over it and shut the glazed eyes. Then he stood up and in horror ran out of the forest in search of help.

I cut it perfectly. He wasn't there...

Then he was there?

...suddenly, out of nowhere.

I knew Pieter had the habit of checking the intended landing spot of each tree before he felled it. Once he waited for an hour to let a somnambulant hedgehog waddle out of danger's path. The tree that killed Erwin was destined to be left on the forest floor as compost. It had a parasitic ivy vining up its bark, rot running through the core. Pieter glanced over and waited for his brother to get out of the way, made an all-clear sign and waited for one in return, and then he nestled his shoulder into the trunk and sliced through the last remaining hinge of wood. What he saw when he looked up was impossible. Time

Life goes on, Pieter said.

Even then, in the rawness of our loss, a transformation was taking place. The gap was closing in. We were quietly re-forming ourselves, nurturing aspects within ourselves and in each other that reminded us of Erwin. We were compensating, filling in the spaces he had occupied. Slowly, invisibly, he was returning to us by our sheer willingness to have him here.

I should have gone up to his room, with its unadorned simplicity — a waif walking naked through the damp chill and dark, willing the body warmth of my first bed to carry me to my second. I imagine the sex would have been rough and primal and seeking only the most primitive of human outlets, a speedy orgasm. It would be merely the closing of a circle, defining a part of my real relationship.

Pieter and I were still waiting for the crane in this godforsaken landscape, when I headed off into the destruction, hopping tree trunks and shimmying beneath giant, fallen trees until I was sure I was out of sight of the road and any other little hovel, barn, or house. I needed to find a secluded spot where I could take a shit. In the beginning, I'd found it awkward, this shitting in the midst of civilization. I judged wind direction and tried wherever possible, if not to hold it, to crap downwind. As time passed I sloughed off these concerns and acquiesced to my body; by then Erwin, had come to work in the forest with us. One night as the evening dark descended, Pieter, Erwin and I shat simultaneously, a trilogy, a trinity of defecation, calling encouragement from our separate spots across another tree-strewn farmer's field.

Soil of God, I said.

Take away the sins of the world, said Erwin.

Amen, added Pieter.

We marked our piles of crap with deadfall sticks from the trees we had cut that day, branches that the local people would later collect and bundle into faggots for their woodstoves and fireplaces. I wonder now if they might have come upon our dumps as they worked and expressed their offence with shock and disgust, but I didn't think about that then. Pieter made the sign of the cross in the air — his thick workman's hand over the mound of feces.

In nomine dictum, strontium heilige aarden in Gloria, Aaa-men. Shit, holy earth. Glorious father in the heavens. Aaa-men.

From my contrived wilderness privy, now, I could see Pieter surveying the destroyed forest. Behind him the nuclear chimney was like a decapitated minaret, the thin line of drifting smoke the only sign of its true purpose. Its grey concrete austerity had a monastic stillness; the forest, too, was still that morning, except for the creatures skittering about in search of safe haven. The light at that time of the year rarely opened up the sky but skimmed the clouds and bounced away back upwards. It was a diffusion — the edges of the rain-threatening clouds were a perplexing, pollution-build-up yellow. I made my way back to him over and under the felled forest.

A farmer had hobbled by. He was a small, bent, elderly man with lines etched on the lines in his face, the onset of cancer splotched along his nose, and rot flourishing in his few remaining teeth. He wore blue rubber clompen; smears of fodder and dung from the morning rounds covered his overalls. When he saw me heading over, he tipped his cap, h'lo.

Hi.

He glanced out at the destruction.

Whad'ya know? he said, turning back to Pieter.

It's a job, said Pieter.

Better you than me. Stront werk, that's what it is.

The winds had raged with such a ferocity that the earth seemed to react sympathetically to our loss. At the peak of the storm, Pieter and I had huddled in bed. Seeking warmth or unity, we made love, a lick from the neck down and down to his penis. A bumblebee slammed itself repeatedly into our bedroom window, so we let it in. It nestled into a warm corner of the frame, making a confused effort to sting the glass.

Pathetic fallacy, I had said
It's not so bad, said Pieter.
Not you, I said.

We lived in an old manor house on the Prinsenhof. The tower spire on the old beer-hops factory attached to the house pierced the gathering sky. It was wrought for beauty more than function and would totter and fall as the winds reached their height. I wished the bee was Erwin slamming into the window, trying to come back. Even if he was only a bee, he could sting, make honey, let us know he was all right, alive.

I used to bring coffee up to Erwin in bed and wake him up by placing my cold hand on his sleep-warmed shoulder. He twitched me away as a horse does an insect, with a neural shiver. His eyes opened as the smell of coffee registered, and he smiled. His light blue eyes had the translucent quality of a sub-equatorial ocean. They gave off a buoyancy that is hard to describe.

Thank you, he said.

Is it good?

I sat next to him on his bed and marvelled at his beauty, at the pure awakening loveliness of him. We chatted in English, laughing at the way he put words together, more and more and more words in a hopeless attempt at meaning. I could easily have slid under the covers, my body curving into his, our skin rising excitedly to the touch; I did not.

Oh my god, I said to Pieter one night early on. He's better than you in every way.

Maybe not every way, Pieter said, sliding his hand between my legs, fingers searching through the wet. As children, Pieter and Erwin had been inseparable. Their mother had even dressed them identically, despite the fact that they were born a year apart. The familiarity of their brotherliness was reassuring to me (what returns a touch might have, now he's lost?).

Pieter and I went to bed when our eyes sunk closed at the table from reading, the wine having seeped into our dreams even, and we would huddle up close on the makeshift bed installed where an ancient toilet had once been. We were desperate to draw heat from one other in the frigid coastal humidity. We would murmur love adages in broken languages, and we would fuck. Loudly clipping each stair with his feet, Erwin would go upstairs to his room, where he occasionally had a houseguest but most nights didn't. I would think about him making the lonely trip there to his cold, empty bed. Stupidly, I was unable to fathom the way in which his loneliness was a creation of our union.

There is a photograph I took of Erwin and Pieter. They are singing together in the yellow light of a dozen candles, the woodstove open for still more light. Pieter and Erwin are leaning into one another, both wearing rust-coloured sweaters knit by old girlfriends, canvas caps — the light turning these to haloes around their heads. If I suspend my disbelief, time stops there. They look, even on close inspection, like Siamese twins. I said this once to Erwin as we stood about in the forest one day, waiting for Pieter to fell more trees so that we could de-branch them. Erwin was smoking and swatting at me playfully with his wool scarf, wrapping the scarf around my legs and trying to trip me.

You are like Siamese twins, you and Pieter.
What's so good about the Siamese?
You know, Siamese twins are joined in body.
Ha, he said, yes. We could be joined at your hip.

I knew how to examine a branch on a felled tree and expertly remove it. Sometimes this involved slicing twice or more, sometimes from below, the chainsaw blade cutting along the curve here and then there; the tree would almost sigh as it was relieved from the tension in which that branch held it, and then it would shift into a calmer position. We cleared each forest as if we were in a ballet, dancing around each other, making short work of each tree until the field lay littered with branches, and the crane or the skidder could pull our immaculate logs into an ever-growing pyramid.

Three hundred cubic metres per day. It's amazing, I said.

Each day a little more, said Erwin.

No. There must be a threshold. If you go too fast, the pattern will be disrupted and it will lack beauty.

So?

It isn't worth it, then, I said.

What's beautiful about a felled forest?

Something. Something unspeakable.

In this hurricane-hurled forest, Pieter and I trimmed branches, some huge and twisted, while we waited for the crane. There was no sense trying to cut the roots away without some mechanical help — far too dangerous. We checked the length of the tree before we sliced through the leader to make sure the trunk was free and straight. And still the cutting bands got caught regularly in the torque-prone stems. We carried wedges and a sledgehammer around with us in order to pry the tree open if it pinched the saw's blade. The stinging nettle hid an assortment of unpredictable miseries, too, including old fencing that nicked the saw's razor edge. We had to stop every couple of trees, take out the files, and sharpen our tools. Meanwhile, Pieter's skin had swollen from the nettle rash. Also, my saw kept cutting out. First it surged, then it coughed and stalled. I opened it up, cleaned the spark plug with an Opinel knife, cut out the exhaust debris. It was a day from hell, as Pieter had predicted.

As I worked, I stood on the trunk of the tree I was cleaning, shifting my weight as the tree rolled or shifted its. A wild ride and chancy. The height and unpredictability of each tree intensified my concentration. I had learned early on to jump at the slightest worrisome movement. I assessed each tree by its particularities — the way the bark turned up its spine, the direction of its fall, what lay on it and in what manner. I could climb along a tree hanging upwards of two metres in the air and work with precision and without fear. There was a thrill to it. Finally, the crane arrived on the back of a flatbed truck. The operator, a hulking giant named Paul, emerged from the cab.

'Dag, said Paul.

'Lo.

As soon as he perceived my gender, Paul began to leer at me. He smiled at me from the glassed-in booth of the crane. Whenever he spotted me and he thought I might be looking, a horny glaze came over his eyes, and he put his hands down between his legs to the gearshift. He sat up high in the red crane, watching me as much as possible while he was working. Later, I would come to thank him.

Paul positioned his crane so that the jaws held the tree stem. Pieter stood as far back as he could without losing his balance and sliced through the tree as close to the roots as possible without catching dirt in the chainsaw blade. As often as not, the root ball crashed back to earth right in the spot where it had emerged. The craters were filled. I noticed suddenly that Pieter had lost weight; his pants were loose on him. Thinness gave him the appearance of having grown taller. He had changed even as he regretted the possibility of moving on, changed physically. Soft down had sprouted on his chest, his manner had more room for humour, his lovemaking had become more exploratory. He was approximating Erwin's presence; we both were.

I would die without you, Pieter said to me.

No.

I would drink.

You drink now.

I moved further and further away from the racket of the crane. What must it have sounded like, I wondered, these huge trees ripping up the earth, trees crashing into other trees, splintering with thunderous cracks. Did the small forest creatures under the roots look up, their roofs removed, their vulnerability exposed, and notice death looming with each new crash? The reactor chimney smoke swirled into a mini-twister, thrown this way and that in a smoke dance. I sat down amongst the fallen trees and ate a sandwich that I had stuck in my jacket pocket. It was a squished pair of bread slices with a thick smear of fresh butter, two speculaas cookies in between.

I could no longer see Pieter or the crane. When the buzz of Pieter's saw cut out for any length of time, I counted off the minutes it took for him to roll and smoke a cigarette. If the silence lengthened, I became alarmed, and a bilious anxiety rose in my stomach. He had become everything to me; we were inseparable. Perplexing death images dissipated only when I stood close to Pieter; when we were in bed together I felt complete. The night after the accident, Pieter and I crawled like maimed animals under the duvet. I had sorted his clothing in the upstairs laundry, held the blood-soaked cloth up to my face. I had no idea what I was doing. I had read once that Madame Curie held her husband's brains in a handkerchief for days, not able to bear the loss of his mind. I put one little bloodied wood chip into my mouth (the metallic taste of Erwin melting on my tongue), and then I shoved Pieter's sullied clothes away from me into the washing machine. I watched them agitate clean. I should have built a shrine around them, I thought later, as Pieter whimpered in bed next to me. I was not asleep; I was heartlessly alert when Pieter held me close and made love to me. It was Erwin's face and his body that came to mind.

Does it bother you that I loved him?

I am not a jealous person by nature.

I felt this comment as a heavy burden. It weighed on me. Not as guilt but as something more tangible, as if I were somehow responsible for propping it all up, holding us on the earth. Everything had an enormous heaviness. My legs moving from tree to tree were magnetized and grounded; I could not fall. The Doem laboratories had repatriated loads of vitrified nuclear waste in barrels deep in the ground; they'd dug a series of a hundred tunnels seventy-six metres beneath me, deep under the Tertiary clay that itself created a non-porous shield against any possible leakage. The little fishes bumping into the wire mesh. Erwin's hand on my throat. Even laughter carried weight. I felt the world had a boundlessness that I could not escape. And this depressed me.

Even sorrow is fleeting, Pieter said.

That's not my experience.

The crane operator was the closest when I fell. He clambered out of his machine, as quickly as his giant body allowed, to help me. I had screamed. Pieter was further away and took longer to arrive. Paul's hands were enormous, like grizzly paws. They lifted me as if I were a bundle of dried sticks. I had been listening to the sweet whine of Pieter's saw off to my left and back. I had looked up into the sky before giving the tree my full attention. There was a single bird grappling with the air currents. It spun midair and regained flight balance, seeming to enjoy the inevitability of its own weakness. I looked carefully along my tree, and I sliced it through. The tree became an instant catapult, grabbing me by the midsection. It hurled me in seeming slow motion in an arc some ten metres through the air before I dropped at full force into another log, spine first. I expected to die and braced myself for this inevitability. I held the spinning blade of the chainsaw as far away from my body as possible, reasoning that if I dropped the tool it might cut me in half. The space around my eyes in that instant of airborne thrust was shattered into a million quartz-like shards. In the strange expansion of time before I landed (the awful shock of pain; the catapulting tree flinging about trying to find its central calm), I sought to explore these gem-like splinters, their texture, their variegated edges, and imagine a way they might fit together to explain to me what I had become, and then wonder whether, if given the time, I could look through this clear stone of my creation to determine what had become of us.

KATHRYN KUITENBROUWER is the author of the bestselling novel *All the Broken Things* and the novels *Perfecting* and *The Nettle Spinner*. She is also the author of the short story collection *Way Up*. Her writing has won a Danuta Gleed Award, the Sidney Prize (USA), and has been nominated for the Amazon.ca/Books in Canada First Novel Award and the ReLit Award. Her short fiction has appeared in *Granta Magazine*, *The Walrus,* and *Storyville*. She has taught and mentored students through The New York Times Knowledge Network, The University of Toronto School of Continuing Studies, and the University of Guelph MFA in Creative Writing. Kathryn has recently completed a residency at Yaddo and a fellowship at the Virginia Centre for the Creative Arts.

Copyright © 2003, 2014 by Kathryn Kuitenbrouwer.

All rights reserved. No part of this work may be reproduced or used in any form or by any means, electronic or mechanical, including photocopying, recording or any retrieval system, without the prior written permission of the publisher or a licence from the Canadian Copyright Licensing Agency (Access Copyright). To contact Access Copyright, visit www.accesscopyright.ca or call 1-800-893-5777.

Series edited by Martin James Ainsley.
Cover and series design by Chris Tompkins.
Art direction and page design by Julie Scriver.
Printed in Canada.
10 9 8 7 6 5 4 3 2 1

Library and Archives Canada Cataloguing in Publication

Six@sixty / edited by Martin James Ainsley.

Short stories compiled to commemorate Goose Lane's sixtieth anniversary.
5. What had become of us / Kathryn Kuitenbrouwer.
Issued in print and electronic formats.
ISBN 978-0-86492-853-5 (set : pbk.).—ISBN 978-0-86492-793-4 (set : epub).—
ISBN 978-0-86492-860-3 (v. 5 : pbk.).—ISBN 978-0-86492-736-1 (v. 5 : epub).

I. Ainsley, Martin James, 1969-, editor. II. Kuitenbrouwer, Kathryn, 1965- . What had become of us.

PS8321.S59 2014   C813'.010806   C2014-902978-0
                                    C2014-903186-6

Goose Lane Editions acknowledges the generous support of the Canada Council for the Arts, the Government of Canada through the Canada Book Fund (CBF), and the Government of New Brunswick through the Department of Tourism, Heritage, and Culture.

Goose Lane Editions
500 Beaverbrook Court, Suite 330
Fredericton, New Brunswick
CANADA E3B 5X4
www.gooselane.com

This book, typeset in Minion Pro
and Gill Sans, was printed and bound in Canada by
Friesens in Altona, Manitoba, on 55 lb. Rolland Enviro
100 FSC Natural Antique.